The
Shifting
Heart

# The Shifting Heart

## Richard Beynon

Angus & Robertson Publishers

Angus & Robertson Publishers
London ● Sydney ● Melbourne ● Singapore
Manila

First published by Angus & Robertson Publishers, Australia, 1960
First school edition 1969
Reprinted 1970, 1971, 1972, 1973 (*twice*), 1974
This A & R Playtexts edition 1976

© Richard Beynon 1960

National Library of Australia
card number and ISBN   0   207   13327   1

PRINTED IN AUSTRALIA BY WATSON FERGUSON AND CO., BRISBANE

For

MR. LECZYCKI

Who need not have died that Christmas. . . .

## List of Characters

Poppa Bianchi

Leila Pratt

Gino Bianchi

Momma Bianchi

Clarry Fowler

Maria Fowler

Donny Pratt

Detective-Sergeant Lukie

# ACT I

*It is four o'clock; and Christmas Eve in Collingwood.*

*Collingwood, which once composed most of the early city of Melbourne and since, has steadily decomposed.*

*We see now the last of a terrace row; the back yard in fact, of the house belonging to Mr. and Mrs. Vicenzo Bianchi. The yard is untidy with a large garbage can down* L. *The overflow from this is contained in a small household bucket, and about these the ground lies in bald, untended patches. The whole is bound tightly by two paling fences—one on either side of the stage. The one to the right forms an almost formidable barrier; a length of barbed wire even running along its top. The left fence relaxes with an air of friendly dilapidation, and in the winter the boards set up a moan as they swing on rusted nails. Following this fence, a side-entrance runs upstage and out of sight to the front of the house. This provides normal entrance to the house . . . the front street entrance being reserved for strangers or to impress guests.*

*The porch or back veranda—is in full view, with a wire door centre back. Enter it: turn right and you are in the kitchen; left, you've reached the Bianchi's dining-room. In summer their bedroom is the veranda which explains the iron bedstead clinging to the veranda to the right side of the wire door. Above the roof we can see two windows. A small one above the kitchen belongs to the bathroom. A larger one over the dining-room gives light to the room belonging to their son; Gino.*

*[It is four o'clock. The sun is still positive.* POPPA BIANCHI *sits at the foot of the two steps leading down from the porch to the yard; his backside saved from the earth by a cushion, another one at his back as he rests against the "built-up" veranda. He plays on a harmonica—not expertly but with ambitions. "Santa Lucia" is his choice, because the melody is simple . . . until he reaches the "high middle bit" which he muffs; goes back; tries again; muffs again . . . and, dismissing it, jumps quickly on to the last line. Then carefully, he starts again.*

*He is interrupted when a moment later, something sails over the fence* R. *and lands in the yard. He crawls down; and picks up the remains of a once-healthy fish. He looks at the fence* R. *lifts the harmonica to his lips and begins to play:*

> Once a jolly swagman camped by a billabong,
> Under the shade of a coolibah tree . . .

*Tho' not intentional, the playing has a plaintive sadness about it; an error of adjustment. The melody is interrupted when the wire door from the next house cracks shut, and as she hangs out her washing a woman's strident voice tentacles over the fence* L. *singing:*

> I'm dreaming of a white Christmas . . .
> With every Christmas card I write. . . .
> May your days be merry, and . . . oooooooooowh!*

POPPA *grinningly grimacing at the lack of both tune and feeling, has, with a flick of the wrist sent the fish sailing over the* L. *fence landing it home right on cue. There is a deathly pause. Then a face appears over fence* L. *It is* LEILA PRATT.

LEILA [*flatly*]. Did you lose something?

POPPA. Mmmmmm? Oh . . . hello, Mrs. Pratt.

LEILA. Never mind: hello. [*She holds up the fish.*] Friend a yours?

POPPA. Mmmmmm? How you come to get that, uh?

[LEILA *waits patiently for an explanation.*

[*Innocently*]. But . . . I threw it there . . . [*Indicating the garbage can*]. How it come to find you, uh?

LEILA [*calls*]. Mrs. Bianchi?

POPPA. No; no; no; you don't tell momma. It's my little joke, that's all.

LEILA. Joke, you call it! Look at them bones; you coulda hooked me rotten eye out.

POPPA. Oh, Mrssa Pratt you know I wouldn't do nothing like a that; 'S Christmas spirit, uh?

LEILA. Christmas spirit's right with fish all over your washing. Thought you didn't eat fish anyway.

POPPA. We don't, but [*He indicates the fence* R.]

LEILA. What; you mean she threw it over?

[POPPA *shrugs. This is an old war.*

LEILA. The stinking bitch! [*She hauls back to throw it.*]

POPPA. No; no; no, please! We don't want no trouble.

LEILA. You! You're too soft, I tell you. *You* keep taking it, *she'll* keep giving it.

POPPA. All right, all right, one day we talk, but not today. Today's Christmas.

LEILA [*dropping the fish on top of the overstuffed garbage can on his side of the fence*]. Well, here's your present back.

[*She disappears.* POPPA *wanders back to his cushions, and a*

[9]

*moment later* LEILA, *simply by pushing two boards aside, steps into the yard.*

LEILA. Going away?

POPPA. You know, momma. Home is home; and just now with Maria . . .

LEILA. Trouble? Again?

POPPA. No; no trouble but . . . we all be glad when it's over.

LEILA. By the look of her y'aint got long to wait.

POPPA. She's big, uh? [*He giggles.*] Maybe twins. To make up for the last time, uh?

LEILA. If you're thinking *that* way, we'll have to make it triplets.

POPPA [*he joins his hands together in supplication*]. Please God, no more like that. I didn't think we could take a more like that. [*He brightens.*] But now we don't have to. Three times lucky, uh?

LEILA. Touch wood.

POPPA. Toucha wood; yeah. She don't deserve all this, Maria. She's a good girl. Multo bravo . . . You don't know her before we come here. She grow up so quick—clever too. At twenty, that's all, twenty she comes to momma: momma, she say: Italia finito. For you's maybe good. For me; for Gino [*He shakes his head.*] So first I go. Go, she say! We say to her: wherea you go, Rome? Napoli? Australia, she say. Then we don't even know where Australia is. If's good, she say you come too . . . and bring Gino. Gino always she look after like her own baby. . . . And so she leave us, and here she comes; alone, not a soul she knows. 's brave, uh? 's *multo* bravo.

LEILA [*absorbed*]. Trying to think what *I* was doing at twenty. [*She shrugs it off.*] Oh, well, it's too hot for regrets.

POPPA. You aska Maria; she don't regret. She don't come here, she don't meet Clarry. No Clarry, no bambino.

[*He shrugs and begins to play.*

LEILA. Yeah, and no waking us up every morning with you yelling at Gino. Look, it's bad enough having the blurter from the factory. . . .

POPPA. Who yells?

LEILA. You don't believe *me*: ask her. [*She indicates the fence* R.] In the butcher's this morning, was she going on about youse. Noisy, smelly, untidy. I tell you: if she leads the revolution, you'se'll be the first to go. Where *is* the big boy, anyway?

POPPA. Gino? Too early for Gino. He's the working man.

LEILA. Working man, eh? Lover boy, too from what I hear. Collingwood's Casanova.

POPPA. Casanova? Ah, Casanova I understand. [*He chuckles.*] Poppa too, was Casanova. Where you hear this?

LEILA. Mmm . . . he goes to the dance on Saturday nights, doesn't he?

POPPA. Si. [*Grinning.*] And the girls: they *like* to dance with him, uh?

LEILA. Not only dance, neither.

POPPA. Not only . . .? [*He starts to chuckle.*] Ooooooh . . .'s good. Not only dance, huh? That's good: that's good: that's very good. [*He nudges* LEILA *who begins to chuckle too : and soon both are roaring with laughter. Then she checks and sniffs.*]

LEILA. What's that smell?

POPPA. Hmmmmm?

LEILA. Smell?

POPPA. [*sniffs*]. I don't smell.

LEILA. Down there. [*Suspiciously.*] Did you put your rubbish tins out yesterday?

POPPA. [*naively*]. I forget.

LEILA. Ah—look. Honest she's right, you know: one of these days you're gonna wake up and find the Health Inspector on your mat. I mean, get the wind in the right quarter, it's going to be a snifter Christmas for us, isn't it?

POPPA. I tell you; if's bad, you come in here. We give you such a good time you don't even notice.

LEILA. Ta, I can just see Donny diving into a plate of spaghetti for his Christmas dinner!

POPPA. Why you think . . .? Always you think we eat spaghetti.

LEILA. Well, every time I see you you seem to be wound up in it.

POPPA. But not today. Today Clarry comes, Maria comes. To-morrow Clarry's momma; then there's Gino, there's momma, and there's me . . . and there's; what you think? [*Momentously.*] Turkey!

LEILA. Dinkum?

POPPA. The biggest, fattest tremendousus turkey you ever seen. Plenty for us; plenty for you; for everyone.

LEILA [*flatly*]. We got a piece of pork.

POPPA. Ooooh; for Christmas? That's not good.

LEILA. Arsenic'd be worse; and he'd deserve it. Every rotten Christmas; you've seen him; so stinking he doesn't even know what he's eating. I'll slice it up thin and tell him it's poultry. [*She pushes herself to her feet.*] Ah well, as the loose-living monk said: back to the habit. Every Christmas . . . the same old thing . . . on and on . . . like . . .

POPPA. Sssss; you hear something?

LEILA. Mmmmmm?

[12]

POPPA. In the house. Someone comes in the house. [*He calls.*] Anyone's there?

LEILA [*after a pause*]. Front door open?

POPPA. Sure; so we get the breeze.

GINO [*calling off*]. It's all right, momma; it's only me.

POPPA [*to* LEILA]. You see? [*Calling.*] Gino . . .? [LEILA *returns through the fence.*]

GINO [*offstage*]. That *you*, Poppa?

POPPA. Where are you? What do you do home so early?

GINO [*flings up the upstairs* R. *window and leans outs*]. Where's momma?

POPPA. Never mind; where's momma. What you do sneaking in the front way?

GINO. The front door was open, poppa, so . . .

POPPA. So never mind the door was open. You think your momma polish the floor just so you can make it dirty?

GINO. I didn't make it dirty.

POPPA. Why you don't use the sideways like always, uh? Answer me. You not in no trouble?

GINO [*laughs*]. Trouble? Me? I don't know what that word means; you ask Mrs. Pratt. Hi, Mrs. Pratt.

LEILA [*her head appearing over the fence*]. Ask me what?

GINO. How's my best girl today, uh?

POPPA. You don't be so cheeky.

GINO [*seriously*]. Cheeky, Poppa. What you say? We're friends. Me and Mrs. Pratt; we're friends. [*Then gaily.*] Hey, Mrs. Pratt what about you come to the dance with me tonight, uh?

POPPA. Dance; dance. . . .

GINO. Not just a dance tonight; no; A Ball. Huh? Big Ball.

[13]

LEILA. Don't think me old pins'd stand up to it, Gino.

GINO. Oooooh, pretty girl like you. Plenty of life to you, yet. I got plenty of money, I give you a good time.

LEILA. Take a tip kid, don't go flashing your money around up there, or some of those larrikins'll be giving *you* a good time.

POPPA. Yeah, you listen to that. What you do with Clarry, anyway?

GINO. Uh? Oh, we finish early so he drop me in Town. He's gone home to pick up Maria.

POPPA. What for he drop you in Town?

GINO. Always the questions.

POPPA. What you do in Town?

GINO. I don't do nothing. I want to buy something.

POPPA. You got too much already. What you want to buy? [GINO *opens his mouth to remonstrate.*] I want to know.

GINO. I want to buy—a new ball dress for my best girl, eh, Mrs. Pratt? [*He disappears.*]

POPPA [*shouting*]. You answer me funny, one of these days, you see, I kicka your backside so hard you got two dents.

[*At this moment an anguished voice tears down the sideway.*

MOMMA [*offstage*]. Poppa! Poppa! Come quick!

POPPA. 'S momma! All right. All right, Momma; 's all right. I come.

[*He exits running up the sideway. There are garbled voices, and after a few moments an irate* POPPA *storms down the sideway carrying a bottle of sauce. He is followed by* MOMMA—*laden with shopping.*

POPPA. You wanna to frighten me to death, that's what you wanna to do. And for what? Lousy bottle of sauce!

[14]

MOMMA [*wearily*]. I tell you; from under my arm it was slipping.

POPPA. I don't care . . .!

MOMMA. You care if it fall and break and you gotta to buy another bottle.

POPPA [*holds out the bottle and deliberately lets it drop*]. It fall. So it breaks? NO! So what for you scream a like this?

MOMMA. I don't scream.

POPPA. She don' . . .? [*He turns to* LEILA.] Mrs. Pratt . . .?

MOMMA. Aaaah, Mrs. Pratt. I don't see you. Hot, uh? My sing-a-let, it feels like a wet face-a-flannel.

POPPA [*to* LEILA]. You were here! Does she scream, or don' she? [LEILA *opens her mouth but is forestalled*.] You call Mrs. Pratt a liar? Mrs. Pratt, she thought you was dying.

MOMMA. Dying? Oh . . . you don't get rida me so easy. [*To* LEILA.] Mr. Wilson, I think he go soon. You see him today? Oooh, he's got his twitch a back, worse than ever.

POPPA. You don't mind Mr. Wilson's twitch, you minda me.

MOMMA. 'S hot, Poppa; my arms ache. You take these things in the kitchen, uh?

POPPA [*reluctantly*]. You don't deserve it.

MOMMA. I know, I know. But just now I like to sit down a minute.

POPPA. You feel okay?

MOMMA. I feel okay. You take these, mm?

POPPA. You feel okay? You sure?

MOMMA [*nicely*]. Poppa, you *don't* take these things soon, I throw them at you.

[POPPA *moodily takes the parcels.*

POPPA. And another thing you don't deserve: good husband like me. [*He exits.*]

MOMMA. Yeah; yeah; good husband, poppa, good husband. [*To* LEILA] 'S too hot to argue. Mr. Wilson? Why he twitch? Why he twitch a like that, uh? I know; I know, you say, but lotsa people they drink, they don't all twitch.

LEILA. They don't all drink plonk.

MOMMA. Plonk?

LEILA. Plink. That's his trouble.

MOMMA. Plink? What'sa plink?

LEILA. Plonk. Half-the-price. Twice-the-strength. Try it. No time you'll be twitching with the best of 'em.

MOMMA. 'S a shame. All the way home I think, what sorta Christmas for him to sit there and twitch all a time. And he's such a nice man.

> POPPA *reappears on the veranda.*

Every time I go into his shop he gives a little twitch, and what'sa for you today, he says: what'sa for Momma Macaroni?

POPPA. He still calla you that? Bianchi's that's your name. Bianchi; and he know, so why he always calla you this . . . this . . .?

MOMMA. Momma Macaroni? Because he like a me.

POPPA. He don't have to like a you. All he gotta do is serve a you.

MOMMA. Poppa . . .

POPPA. He likes you too? [*To* LEILA].

MOMMA. I feel dry . . .

POPPA [*to* MOMMA]. Then why he don't call her Mrs. Steak and Eggs, uh? No, this is to make a difference, and this I don't like.

MOMMA. You fetch me a drink, uh? Drink. [*Quietly to* LEILA.] He got no understanding.

POPPA. What you say?

MOMMA. No, she don't want one: just me. Nice cool drink.

> [POPPA *exits mumbling into the kitchen.*

You know what Mr. Wilson call him? Poppa Spaghetti. [*She bubbles with laughter.*] 'S Momma Macaroni, and Poppa Spaghetti . . . [*She laughs then becomes suddenly serious.*] You don't tell him. 'S good a man, but no sense a humour.

GINO [*calling offstage*]. Poppa, when momma comes back from up the street . . . [GINO *appears at the upstairs window.*] Poppa, will you tell me, 'cos . . .? Oh, hello Momma.

MOMMA. What you do home so early?

GINO. It's not early no more, Momma. It's coming to five o'clock.

LEILA. Five? Jesus! Me Pork. [*She disappears.*]

MOMMA. Clarry and Maria; they say when they come?

GINO [*nods*]. Early; soon. Momma, you gonna to change?

MOMMA. Change? What for?

GINO. For Christmas, Momma . . .

MOMMA. So's Christmas; we still gotta eat.

GINO [*cajoling*]. Come on; for today, that's all . . . make yourself beautiful, uh?

MOMMA. You make your*self* beautiful, if you like . . .

GINO. But Momma . . .

MOMMA. You got a clean shirt behind your door: but you take it easy you hear me?

> [GINO, *defeated, has disappeared as* POPPA *comes out carrying a glass of fizzing liquid which he hands to* MOMMA *who takes it without question.*

[17]

'Cos from now to New Year, no more washing. [*She drinks.*] Momma, too, wants the holiday. [*Looking then, from the glass to* POPPA.] What'sa this?

POPPA. Fruit saline.

MOMMA. Fruit saline? You know what fruit saline do to me.

POPPA [*coming into the yard*]. What's he do, uh . . .? [*Calling up to* GINO's *window.*] Alla time up there. You got something to hide?

MOMMA. And that's another thing: you don't yell so much at Gino.

POPPA. Me? Yell?

MOMMA [*gives a healthy burp and holds up the glass.*] Now you see; my stomach complains. (*And she goes back to the conversation: pointing to the* R. *fence.*] She don' like it: I don't like it: Gino don't like it: so you don't yell.

POPPA. Sometimes he make a saint yell.

MOMMA. We don't talk religion; you just don't yell. [*She sniffs.*] What'sa that smell?

POPPA. Smell?

MOMMA. Smell.

POPPA. I . . . er . . . don' a smell. [*He watches as* MOMMA *is drawn to the garbage can.*]

MOMMA. I aska you special to put these out before Christmas.

POPPA. I forget.

MOMMA. Forget! One day . . .! [*She sees the fish.*] What's this?

POPPA. Little present. [*He jerks his thumb at the fence* R.]

MOMMA. She throw this? [POPPA *nods.* MOMMA *jerks up her sleeves.*] Get me the broom.

POPPA. Broom? What for?

MOMMA. The broom! I show you what for.

> [MOMMA *dislodges the last foot from one of the fence palings, and taking newspaper from bed begins to roll it into balls.*

POPPA. What you gonna to do?

MOMMA [*thrusting her arm through the fence*]. I gotta first . . . to lift this lid off.

POPPA. Lid? What lid?

MOMMA. The broom: give.

POPPA. No; I don' like this.

MOMMA. Give; give, I say!

POPPA. No; no . . . first you tella me what for you want it.

MOMMA [*with animal enjoyment*]. You see this pipe? Goes through to her drains. We pack it tight with this. [*She indicates the newspaper triumphantly.*] When they pulla the chain . . . she block.

POPPA. What?

MOMMA. They gotta learn a lesson; I teach them. [*She reaches for the broom.*]

POPPA. No, Momma . . . No! You want to get us into prison?

MOMMA. Give! Give, I say!

> [*They struggle audibly for possession of the broom.*

POPPA. Momma, listen, listen . . . this no' right, Momma. No' right what you do.

MOMMA [*heated*]. Right? Is right they send their stinking fish over to us? Their stinking fish they can keep. *And* their cabbage and the rest. Look, look, if we do something they no like, why they don't come and tell us nice like Mrs. Pratt, uh? But no! Never . . . not in eight years we been here, they don't

[19]

say not one word. Instead phfft . . . [*She gestures an over-the-fence throw.*] . . . and you know why? Because they jealous; yeah, because Gino works hard and we pay for our own house, and still they have to pay for their rent. So phfft . . .! Well, that to me's dirty. All right, they play dirty, we play dirty.

POPPA. Not like this, Momma; this is childish.

MOMMA. Oooooh, to my face you don't like just because someone call me Momma Macaroni; but behind my back someone do this, and this you take. That's not to be childish, Poppa, that's to be lunatic.

> [*She exits into the kitchen. Thoughtfully* POPPA *takes out the mouth-organ from his pocket and runs a vacant scale. Finds the sound soothing . . . and begins to play. A moment, then* MOMMA *opens the wire door. Her hat is still on as she secures her apron.*]

MOMMA. And that's funny! Look at you. Look. Hours you play to yourself on that foof-foof thing, and you call *me* childish!

> [*She disappears into the kitchen . . . as* CLARRY *enters down the sideway. He is a rugged man of 36 . . . could obviously manage without help in a fight—but he rarely fights. His aggressiveness comes out only in the presence of emotion. To him, that is a sign of weakness.*]

CLARRY [*listening for a moment*]. You're on the improve, boy.

POPPA. Clarry . . .!

CLARRY. Larry Adler'll have to watch his step.

POPPA. Aaaah, she comes slow; very slow. You know what worries me? The middles. Beginnings I can manage, and the ends, but the middles; you wouldn't believe the trouble I have with the middles.

CLARRY. Eh, I thought you was gunna get this veranda fixed.

POPPA. Ah, it's strong enough; 's tired, that's all.

CLARRY. Yeah, like you, boy. What about that coat of paint you promised it?

POPPA. That was months ago. l paint it months ago, it's just as dirty today. What'sa the good?

CLARRY. If they're all like you, Pop, no wonder the Roman Empire packed up.

POPPA. I paint it sometime. Hey, where's Maria?

CLARRY. She . . . wasn't quite ready. She's coming on by train.

POPPA. Alone?

CLARRY. Why not? Think she'll get lost?

POPPA. No; no. Fairfield's not that far, I know, but . . .

CLARRY. Train's a damn' sight more comfortable, anyway. [*He rubs his seat.*] Springs in the front seat of that truck's like sitting on tweezers.

POPPA. And now, now's the time she gotta take it easy. Looks like this time she's gonna to make it, uh? I know, Clarry, to lose a baby's bad . . .

> [CLARRY *moves to pick up the Gladstone bag he has brought.*

CLARRY. Two, pop. *Two* false alarms we've had. I'm not counting chickens any more.

POPPA. But for those times there was a reason, Clarry.

CLARRY. Reckon?

POPPA [*cheerfully picking up the bag*]. Anyway, three time's lucky, uh? Hey, Hey, what you got in here?

CLARRY. Easy; easy. You want to crack me Christmas presents?

POPPA. Christmas presents? One guess; one guess I bet I know what you buy for Gino. Book, uh? Right?

[21]

CLARRY. That's what he asked for.

POPPA [*nods*]. Like always. Clarry, while the others don't hear; you and me, uh? We . . . [*He shrugs.*] You like Gino, uh, Clarry?

CLARRY [*warily*]. Yeah. He's a good enough kid . . . if he's left alone. Why?

POPPA. He's a good worker, too, uh?

CLARRY. Not much of him; but he's willing.

POPPA [*grins*]. I remember when he first start to work with you on the truck. Even then you say what a good worker he is. But then he's young, and what you say is right: first he has to learn the business and then afterwards, maybe . . . you remember what you say afterwards?

CLARRY [*slight pause*]. Did he tell you to tackle me like this?

POPPA. Gino? Oh Clarry, you know him better than that. Anything he want you to know, he tell you straight because he respect you. Because one day he wanna be the man you are. [*Simply.*] That boy, Clarry, he loves you.

CLARRY. Beats me why you don't plant . . . carrots or something down here.

POPPA [*grins and shakes his head*]. Clarry: like all the rest: you so afraid. [*Quickly as* CLARRY *turns to attack.*] Not afraid no. Maybe that's no right; ashamed, uh? But not of the bad things: always the good. 'S funny that.

CLARRY [*gently*]. You want to hang on to your wind, Pop. You'll need it all for your mouth-organ.

POPPA. Uh? All right: so I minda my own business. But . . Clarry, you know this dance place he goes? You think this a good place? ·

CLARRY. Why?

POPPA [*seriously*]. They fight there, Clarry.

CLARRY. Nah . . .

POPPA. Yeah, yeah, they do. And you know, nine a times outa ten it's not the local boys who fights—not each other; it's always with boys like . . . boys with *names* like . . . Gino. This' why all the time I think to keep him busy. Give him the responsibility; so he don't have no *time* to go *wrong*. [*He laughs suddenly.*] Every week, Clarry, every week he goes to the bank. You know how much he got? Don't tell him I tell a you . . . but I see his book. He's got . . . well, maybe I *don't* tell you . . . but it's enough; enough for a down payment, 'cos just lately one time—two, maybe, he says about a little truck. Ooooh, I can justa see the big sign: Fowler *and* Bianchi. Good, uh? And together you clean up all the scrap metal in the whole town; whole State, maybe.

CLARRY. Careful, Pop, careful; you'll be taking off.

POPPA. Me? I don't take off; my brains she's too little. But you . . .! You got your contacts already . . .

CLARRY. Yeah, enough to keep one truck working.

POPPA. And these people, they tell other people, and when Gino has *his* truck, you see: you get so many orders you got to buy *another* truck for *me*; and then momma has a truck and . . .

CLARRY. It wouldn't work, Pop.

POPPA. Wouldn't work?

CLARRY. I mean: times change. Like, I was pretty green myself then; so was the scrap metal business. In the last five years it's grown into a pretty profitable business, you know, and when business starts getting profitable, that's when throats get cut.

POPPA. You mean . . .?

CLARRY. I mean, Gino makes a good living. We both do. And

[23]

we like working the same truck together. Why break up a good team?

POPPA. You mean: you don't want him no more as partner?

CLARRY. Three square meals—and a pint of cream, that's all 1 want, Pop, and no trouble.

POPPA. Trouble? But . . .?

MOMMA [*from inside*]. Clarry? Clarry's that you?

CLARRY. Doesn't miss a trick, does she?

POPPA. But, Clarry; what trouble could boy like Gino make?

CLARRY [*calling to* MOMMA]. And you needn't go talking sweet 'cos there's no presents for anyone this year. You hear? [*He winks at* POPPA.]

POPPA. Clarry . . .?

CLARRY [*calling*]. Except a paira socks for Pop. [*To* POPPA.] Beauties, too. Flame red.

POPPA [*deviated at last*]. Red? For me?

CLARRY. Yeah. Match your eyes. And listen. [*He rattles the bag; bottles clink.*] Half a doz, a' the best; case you burst into flame.

> [POPPA *smiles in spite of himself* CLARRY *moves on to the veranda, as the bathroom window shoots up and Gino leans out.*

GINO. Poppa! Whata we do with ice in the bath?

POPPA. Mmmmmm?

GINO. Ice. There's ice in the *bath*.

POPPA. You don't touch. That's extra—to keep cool.

GINO. But what about my shower?

POPPA. You washed this morning. What you want now with the shower?

GINO. Poppa, I work since this morning. I smell. I STINK!
I *gotta* have a shower.

POPPA. I say; you don't. Finish.

GINO. But, Poppa . . .

POPPA. You leave the ice where it is . . .

GINO. But . . .

POPPA. . . . if a you don't I kicka your backside so hard you . . .

[MOMMA *comes out from the kitchen.*

MOMMA [*calling*]. Gino-O-O-O? [*To* CLARRY.] Ciaou, Clarry.
Hot, uh? [*She is now in the yard talking up to* GINO.] What for
you yell like this?

GINO. Momma; ice; there's ice in the bath! How can I have a
shower when there's . . . ?

MOMMA [*quietly*]. You find a bucket under the sink here in the
kitchen. You put the ice in the bucket while you have your
shower. When you finish your shower you run the colda tap
till the bath's cool again; then you put the ice back. Q.K.?

GINO. O.K., Momma.

MOMMA [*passing* POPPA]. And you; I wanna to talk to, please.

CLARRY [*calling as he comes back into the yard*]. Gino . . . ?

MOMMA [*calling also as she exits followed by* POPPA]. Hurry up
with the shower, you hear me? It's ice we want, not ice *water*.

CLARRY [*calling*]. GINO . . . ?

GINO [*off*]. All right; all right; you think I'm deaf or something?

[*He appears.*] Oh, Clarry. I didn't know you was here already.
I thought you was poppa yelling.

CLARRY. Got a minute?

GINO. I'm just going to have a shower.

CLARRY. That'll keep; come on down.

[25]

GINO. But already, I just got the ice out of the bath.

CLARRY. Come on down.

GINO [*warily*]. Sure. Okay, Clarry. Sure.

> [*There is a pause.* GINO *disappears; after a moment* POPPA'S *head appears at the wire door.*

POPPA. Psss . . . Clarry. You don't tell Gino I look at his bank book, uh?

MOMMA [*calling loudly from inside*]. POPPA! !

> [*He disappears; and a moment later* GINO *comes laughing on to the veranda.*

GINO. Poppa keeps saying: Merry Christmas, Momma; Merry Christmas, Momma, but she won't listen. [GINO *watches* CLARRY.] What's the matter, Clarry. You mad at me for something?

CLARRY [*suddenly*]. What have you been saying to Maria?

GINO. What about, Clarry?

CLARRY. You been running to her with stories?

GINO. Me . . .? What kinda stories, Clarry?

CLARRY. Like you had another fight at the dance last week.

GINO [*sheepish*]. Oh, that . . . No, 1 didn't tell her that.

CLARRY. Look, I'm warning you again; don't lie to me.

GINO [*genuinely hurt*]. When have I ever lie to you, Clarry? When, uh?

CLARRY. All right; you didn't tell her. So how the hell does she know?

GINO. Well—she see my face when it's all puffed up; and she ask me; but I didn't tell her, Clarry! Honest. I tell her I run into a door, Clarry . . . and then . . . she ask me what's the door's name. [*He grins.*] She's too smart for us, Clarry; smart and pretty, too, uh?

CLARRY: Anyway, I don't think you should go to that dance joint any more.

GINO [*surprised*]. Why not?

CLARRY. I don't think you should, that's all. You got plenty of other places you can go.

GINO. I don't want to go to other places. I want to go to this place.

CLARRY. Look, I'm telling you for your own good. If you won't listen . . . okay then; go ahead, buy trouble.

GINO. I don't buy trouble, Clarry. I buy my ticket, that's all. Because I got as much right to be there as the next man.

CLARRY. Just don't go taking that for granted. You saw what happened when you weighed-in your load yesterday. And it wasn't the first time, was it?

GINO [*seriously*]. Clarry, I swear to you, I didn't try to jump no queue.

CLARRY. That's not the point . . .

GINO. You weren't even there; you were having your drink in the pub; and this Barry—he came after us . . . and you're right, he always tries this. He tries to put his load straight on the scales—before us, so I told him . . .

CLARRY. You shouldn'ta told him.

GINO. Why not?

CLARRY. Because he's an older man, that's why. He was in this game before you were even in the country.

GINO. But I was first in the line, Clarry. I was.

CLARRY. Oh, well never mind. Never mind about him; what else did you tell Maria?

GINO. Nothing. Like I say . . . ?

CLARRY. About Collingwood. You told her you hated it. You wanted to move. Go somewhere else.

GINO. Me? No—I don't tell her that. Why should I tell her that? 'Cos I don't want to move. I like Collingwood. I like it, plenty. Ooooh . . . maybe I say I don't stay here for always. Maybe someday I meet up with a nice girl, and . . . [*He grins.*] I don't wanna be an *uncle* all my life. Someday I be a poppa, like you, Clarry . . . and teach *my* boy English; real fair-dinkum, like you teach me. But . . . what's this all about Clarry?

CLARRY. Ah, forget it.

GINO. I didn't do nothing wrong?

CLARRY. Skip it.

GINO. 'Cos I wouldn't do nothing wrong intentional honest, I . . .

CLARRY. Jeez, you're as bad as your old man; *you* can't stop neither. I said: forget it.

GINO. Okay. Can I go now? [CLARRY *looks at him.*] I got a lot to do.

CLARRY. Like dolling up for the dance?

GINO [*nods enthusiastically*]. But tonight's no dance; tonight's something big; something special. Something REAL special. [*He grins.*] I gotta look pretty. [*At the door he checks and turns.*] Clarry, you're sure I didn't do nothing wrong?

CLARRY [*good-naturedly*]. Look, do I have to write you a letter?

[GINO *laughs, turns to meet* MARIA *entering down the sideway.*

GINO. 'Lo Maria.

MOMMA [*calling off*]. Gino . . . ?

[28]

GINO. See you later. [*At the door.*] Oh . . . Maria: I bought a Christmas present for the baby. So little it's hardly a present at all. You wait till you see.

MOMMA [*off*]. Gino? Do you leave the shower running?

GINO. Oh. What, Momma?

MOMMA. Something's dripping down a these stairs.

GINO. Something's dripping . . . Santa Maria! I left the ice on the landing.

> [*He exits.* MARIA *is 34, and shortly expects her first child. Her face, though drawn now through a difficult pregnancy still retains enough good looks to make most people overlook the fact that it is fundamentally a face of character.*

CLARRY [*to* MARIA]. I thought someone said you wasn't coming.

MARIA. Give me six shillings, please.

CLARRY. What for?

MARIA [*going to the steps, she calls*]. Poppa . . .? You there, Poppa?

CLARRY. Here. [*He takes out a* 10/- *note, but pulls back at the last minute.*] What do you say? [*She says nothing; he slaps the note into her hand.*] And they talk about mules!

> [MARIA *stops at the sideways entrance; unseen by her* POPPA *opens the wire door.*

MARIA. All right, Clarry, if it's words you want, I'll say something, and you better listen good, 'cos next time you curse my . . . something dago temper, I warn you, Clarry, it'll cost you more than six shillings for a taxi. [*She exits.* CLARRY *sees* POPPA.]

CLARRY [*uneasily*]. Taxi; hear that? Thinks I'm made of money. [*Pause.*] You in bad, too?

[29]

POPPA [*nods*]. Momma; she takes my harmonica.

CLARRY [*with cynical humour*]. Oh, you're in *real* trouble.

> [*They sit in dejected silence. Suddenly a gay song bursts from the bathroom.* GINO *sings in Italian.*]

POPPA. There he goes. Singing lousy like always.

CLARRY. Mario Lanza's safe, anyway.

> [GINO *hits a high note.*

LEILA [*off*]. Will you turn that radio down? Before I report youse!

POPPA. You see? That's the sort of thing cause a wars. [*Calls.*] Gino . . .? [*The singing continues.*] Gi . . .

> [POPPA *has stormed down into the yard. But as he turns a warning* MOMMA *opens the wire door.*

MOMMA. And what about the potatoes?

POPPA. What about the potatoes?

MOMMA. I a tell you to peel them, not to tickle them. Inside.

> [POPPA *looks helplessly at* CLARRY, *and moves dejectedly into the kitchen.*

MOMMA. Maria's not come yet?

CLARRY. She's paying off the taxi.

MOMMA. Clarry, 's none a my business, I know, but this time so close . . . you gotta be very kind to each other, uh? Uh-uhuhuhuhuh?

CLARRY [*Good-naturedly mimicking her*]. Uhuhuhuhuh?

> [MARIA *re-enters down the sideway.*

MARIA. Hello, Momma.

MOMMA. Maria. Baby. How you feel, uh? You feel good?

MARIA. I feel fine.

[30]

MOMMA. You do. You don't look good. Pasty . . . don't she?

MARIA. It's the heat that's all.

MOMMA. Sure; the heat, that's all. You sit down; uh? No, here . . . Here. Inside's too hot with all the cooking.

MARIA. I'll come and help.

MOMMA. No. No; you stay here. Clarry tella you a funny story, then soon we eat, uh? [*She goes to the door*.] Maria . . . you know what just now your father he calls me? Grandmomma; sounds beautiful. . .

[*She exits into the kitchen. There is a pause.*

CLARRY. What about me change?

[MARIA *comes down and gives it to him. He playfully grabs her wrist.*

MARIA. I'm not in the mood for games, Clarry.

CLARRY [*throws her hand from him*]. Go ahead then, sulk. *Play* Queen'a the lonely hearts. See who gives in first. [*Pause, then he mimics her.*] "I'm not in the mood for games, Clarry." You and Garbo should get together. [*She rises, and he bars her way.*] Want me to apologize, don't you?

MARIA. I want you to get out of the way, that's all.

CLARRY. Ah, go on; go on, run in squealing to momma.

MARIA [*swings on him*]. Look, what gets into you?

CLARRY. Go on, tell her what a stinking husband I am . . .

MARIA. Do you *like* to see us at each other's throats?

CLARRY. In you go; she's waiting.

MARIA. 'Cos I don't think I can . . . honest. [*She quietly breaks down.*]

CLARRY [*after a helpless moment, goes to her; she tries to pull away from him*]. Look, you want a handkerchief don't you? [*She*

[31]

*moves to take it from him.*] Wait a minute; wait a minute;
what do you say first? [*She snatches it.*] Oooooh, whata lovely-
mannered mummy you're gunna be. [*He watches as she dries
her eyes which she quickly does, and moves away. He stops her;
retrieves his handkerchief.*] Hang on. . . .

MARIA. What's the matter?

CLARRY. You've got an eyelash. No, stand still. . . . [*He
manœuvres closer to her.*]

MARIA. Look, if this is a game . . .

CLARRY. No; great big eyelash. . . . [*He moves closer; grins.*]
You should cry more often.

MARIA. I'm not giving in to you, Clarry.

CLARRY. Makes you go all soft round the edges. [*And gratefully,
they are in each others arms.*]

MARIA. You make me sound like a tired old chocolate.

CLARRY [*softly, exploring her face and neck*]. Fruit-and-nut; keep
the change. [*She tries to free herself.*] No, don't crack down on
a man when he's enjoying himself. [*She does; and wearily sinks
into the chair.*] What's the matter?

MARIA [*thinly smiling*]. Try carrying this weight about with *you*
for a change; you'd know better than to ask. Maybe you will
soon.

CLARRY [*straddles the bench beside her*]. If he thinks I'm gunna
walk the floor lovey-doveying at three o'clock in the morning . . .

MARIA. Ooooooh, tough guy. Listen to the big tough guy.

CLARRY. Not tough, no just firm. I wanna be a father, not a
slave.

MARIA [*softens*]. You will be. This time I promise I won't let
you down.

CLARRY. There you go again. Honest darl, sometimes you say
the stupidest things. . . .

MARIA. I wanted them too, Clarry; as much as you. . . .

CLARRY. 'Course you did. . . .

MARIA. But something inside me, just wouldn't let me hold
them.

CLARRY. I know all that, darl; I know; but you keep talking
about it; you make it sound as if it was something you did
deliberate.

> [*She looks at him for a moment of almost pure guilt, then
> smiling she takes his hand and spreads it tenderly over her
> stomach.*

MARIA. You know something? [*Simply.*] He was kicking *again*
this afternoon.

CLARRY. Yeah? [*He grins.*] Carlton may not know it; they just
got a new full-back.

MARIA. I don't care what he is, so long as he's safe and
wanted. . . .

CLARRY [*lost*]. Fancy the little so-and-so kicking so much . . .!

MARIA. That's what I was trying to say this afternoon, about
Gino. . . .

CLARRY [*breaking*]. Hullo, here we go again. . . .

MARIA. No; all I said was . . .

CLARRY. Oh, don't tell me; I know all you said. Look, we've
already had one fight over him today. . . .

MARIA. I don't want to fight. . . .

CLARRY. That's good. . . . Look darl, you're gunna have a kid of
your own to put up with soon. Don't you think it's about time
you left Gino to look after himself? Jeez, I mean: man his age,
it's enough to have *one* mother, let alone two.

MARIA. Man . . . !

CLARRY. He's twenty-one.

MARIA. He's a child, Clarry.

CLARRY. Ah, nuts.

MARIA. A baby.

CLARRY. Jeez, what does he have to do? Expose himself to prove it?

MARIA. Can't you talk without losing your temper, and getting crude?

CLARRY. But honest darl, you're so . . .

MARIA. All right; all right; all right; he's a man. By your standards, he's a man. Finish.

> [*There is a pause.* CLARRY *wanders, then slowly the last remark seeps through.*

CLARRY. What do you mean; by *my* standards?

MARIA. That's how you always judge him.

CLARRY. What's wrong with that?

MARIA. I keep trying to tell you—but that little mind just won't seem to understand.

CLARRY. Look, go easy on that "little mind" stuff. What do you think I am; number one prize deadhead, or something?

MARIA. No, but . . . [*Gently.*] You don't Clarry, honest. To you people are . . . just . . . people; and—well—it's not as easy as that. They're . . .

CLARRY. Different, yeah . . . [*He taps his temple.*] You told me: we're all different. Well, look, to me: a man's a man . . .

MARIA [*quickly*]. If he's Australian!

CLARRY [*confused under pressure*]. If he's Australian, or . . .

MARIA. Italian? [*Pressing hard.*] What if he's . . . between the two?

CLARRY. God, they have been here for eight years! If he's not adjusted by now . . . !

MARIA. No—it's more than that. . . .

CLARRY. And where's the difference, anyway? Just because you got this bug against Collingwood . . . what do we do? We take him to Fairfield, four miles away. . . .

MARIA. It's not the miles, Clarry, it's the minds of these people. Oh, don't think I blame them. It's not their fault they're poor, have to live hard. But if people live hard, Clarry, then they hate hard.

CLARRY. Nobody hates Gino.

MARIA. You'll be telling me next he fights for the exercise.

CLARRY. Every kid fights. It's second nature.

MARIA. How can I make you understand.

CLARRY. Take it easy, now; take it easy.

MARIA. Do you know why he fights? He fights because he's alone; he's alone because he's different. Do you understand what that means: to be alone?

CLARRY. Remember me? Careless Clarry. The only bird in captivity who never saw his own father.

MARIA. Without a father, you still had more than he's got Clarry. You had all this . . . you got it. Up that sideway; walk into the street . . . and all around you you've got minds that think like yours.

CLARRY. You mean they're stunted too: is that what you mean?

MARIA. I didn't mean that at all. [*Simply.*] Only try, Clarry;

[35]

please try; 'cos you're the only hope he's got, and if you give in like the rest. . . .

CLARRY. Give in?

MARIA. You think I don't know.

CLARRY. Dunno what?

MARIA. Why you won't take him into partnership like you promised.

CLARRY. Jeez; another one! What is this; a bloody conspiracy?

MARIA. Please! Don't swear.

CLARRY. All I've heard all day is Gino; Gino; bloody Gino. What's so special about Gino? [MARIA *rises to move away; he turns her roughly.*] Don't run away when I'm talking to you.

MARIA. Don't do that again.

CLARRY. What's so special about Gino?

MARIA. You're hurting me.

CLARRY. I asked you a question!

MARIA. He's a dago, Clarry. A Wop . . . like me! That's what's so special about Gino.

[*A moment, then* MOMMA *comes on to the veranda on her way to the garbage bin . . . she carries a paper full of potato peelings.*

MOMMA. Oooooh . . . it getsa dark, uh? You nota cold, now the sun's going? Clarry, she not a cold, uh?

MARIA. I'm not cold, Momma; I'm fine; just fine.

MOMMA. I gotta laugh; Maria, look. Clarry. I tell a your poppa for being bad he must peel the potatoes, and look. Better we boil the peels and throw away the potatoes. You gotta laugh.

[GINO'S *window goes up, and he leans out.*

GINO. Momma . . . ?

[36]

patch where he falls; blood—there on the ground; and that blood, Clarry, he can't never have again.

[*She vacantly pats* CLARRY'S *chest and goes slowly into the house. He stands for a long moment looking after her. He turns and his eyes stop at the dark stain on the earth. Kneeling he touches it; it is wet. Taking a handful of earth he sprinkles the patch with something approaching gentleness. He will never be able to explain this curious realization dawning within him . . . but from this moment on, people will be more than just . . . people. He rises; clears away the remains of the party. One bottle clinks into the garbage can. He sees the fish, picks it up, lets it slowly drop; another piece of the jigsaw falling into place. He picks up a half-filled bottle, and the glasses, and turns to follow* MOMMA *into the house when a figure appears at the sideway entrance.*

LUKIE. What's the party over?

CLARRY [*tired*]. This is forty-three, mate; you got the wrong house.

LUKIE. Forty-three's what I want.

CLARRY. I don't know you.

LUKIE. Lukie, Detective-Sergeant.

CLARRY. Russell Street? [LUKIE *nods.*] What's wrong with the front door?

LUKIE. Must be force of habit. The wife's just put down a new carpet in the passage at home. Sorta makes the front door obsolete.

CLARRY. What do you want?

LUKIE [*reading from his notebook*]. Gino Guiseppe Vittorio Bianchi—know him?

CLARRY. I should. He . . . he's the wife's brother. Why?

[69]

LUKIE. I just came from the hospital; relax; he's okay. Got a few facts from them; few more from the dance hall. Wondered if there was anything they'd like to tell me this end?

CLARRY. Nothing that'd make much sense. We're just as much in the dark as you are.

[LUKIE'S *eyes drop to the bottle* CLARRY *is nursing*.

Ah, don't take any notice of this. If I was any soberer I'd be a prude.

LUKIE. According to the bloke on the door . . . [*he refers to his notebook*] . . . Young Bianchi left the dance-hall twice.

CLARRY. That'd be right. He came home.

LUKIE. Thirsty.

CLARRY. Mmmmm?

LUKIE [*indicating the bottles by the rubbish cans*]. Natural. Christmas and so on . . . How many would you say he knocked off?

CLARRY. Who? Gino?

LUKIE. Roughly.

CLARRY. Roughly: none. He had a glass of wine or two, that's all . . . He always had a glass of wine with his tea. . . .

LUKIE. So when he left here you'd say he was pretty merry, eh?

CLARRY. Well, he was happy. . . .

LUKIE. Okay then, happy. . . .

CLARRY. Look, if you're trying to make out he was drunk . . .

LUKIE. No; no, not drunk, just . . .

CLARRY. Not even "just". He was a normal kid, that's all, looking forward to a bit of normal Saturday night fun.

LUKIE [*pleasantly*]. I wouldn't call a bloke who tried to bash his way into somewhere he wasn't wanted, I wouldn't call that normal.

[70]

CLARRY. What're you talking about?

LUKIE. I wouldn't call it sensible, either.

CLARRY. What're you talking about: bash his way in?

LUKIE. That's what he tried to do at the dance.

CLARRY. Why should he do that? He's got money. He's been going to that joint for weeks.

LUKIE. This week was different. This week they changed the policy.

CLARRY. How . . . how do you mean?

LUKIE. Well . . . you know this area . . . it's filling up; New Australians everywhere. They like to dance—some of them're not bad, they tell me. Trouble is, they don't get their way, they go all temperamental. Start breaking things up. It was getting expensive, so the management down there took the only course they could and decided to bar 'em altogether.

CLARRY. Yeah? But what's that got to do with Gino? [LUKIE sighs.] I'm asking you.

LUKIE. Well, with a name like Gino Guiseppe Vittorio Bianchi, he couldn't exactly claim to be a native now could he?

CLARRY. He's been here for eight years. He grew up here.

LUKIE. Not quite the same thing, is it?

CLARRY. He naturalized. That *makes* it the same thing.

LUKIE. I dunno. There's a lot of people—I don't say me, mind you, but a lot of others who look on that as . . . well . . . just a formality. A sort of lever, you know, to cash in on privileges that'd otherwise be denied them.

CLARRY. What kind of a squeeze is this?

LUKIE [*shaking his head*]. Rules are rules. They explained nice and peaceful; they told him the first time, and he was sensible; bit of a skirmish . . . but he went away. When he came back again he *wasn't* so sensible, they tell me. Tried to hack his way in with a knife.

CLARRY. A knife?

LUKIE [*holding up his notebook*]. That's what they said.

CLARRY. Ah, pills! The only time that kid ever toted a knife was at the table.

LUKIE. Yeah? I was under the impression that all da . . . Italians carried knives. Thought it was a national trait.

CLARRY. I know yeah, like owning fruit shops and eating spaghetti. [*He impatiently pours a glass of beer.*] You oughta change your library book.

LUKIE. And just a word Jack, *you* ought to try being a little more courteous.

CLARRY. From a copper. That's rich!

LUKIE. I warn you Jack . . .

CLARRY. Look . . .

LUKIE. No, you look. I didn't come here to argue. I got a badge says I don't have to.

CLARRY. I don't care if you've got a caseful. That kid was not drunk!

LUKIE. All right; all right; don't fight me. I'm on your side.

CLARRY. Don't tell me! I know whose side you're on. Look I lived with your kind of thinking since I was born so don't tell me whose side you're on.

LUKIE. What do you mean?

CLARRY. Oh, real hearts and flowers stuff. M for me Mother. That's what I mean. [*Drains glass of beer.*]

LUKIE. Look you better go easy on that stuff.

CLARRY. Go easy he says! I *been* going easy. I've *had* going easy.

LUKIE. What're you talking about, Jack?

CLARRY [*thrusting his hand into* LUKIE's *face*]. That. That! That's what I'm talking about. Blood! [*He stops and the silence is deep.*] Thirty-six go-easy years ... and ... nobody told me it come from human beings. [*He swings on* LUKIE.] Look I gotta tell something to those people in there. I gotta make it sound ... like sense. If I tell 'em he had a knife you know what they'd do? They'd laugh at me. And they'd be right 'cos look, you don't know him ...

LUKIE [*indicating his notebook*]. All I know are the facts ... What they told me down there ... Look it happens all the time: a kid gets a few drinks inside him, comes the bounce, when he gets bounced back he doesn't like it. Who does? But this one's a hot blood by nature, *he* reaches for a knife. [*Overriding* CLARRY.] A man has to defend himself; that's only reasonable.

CLARRY. Reasonable! Did you ...? At the hospital, did you see him?

LUKIE. No, I didn't he was inside, as a matter of fact.

CLARRY. Well I'll tell you. Here, his face was ... practically kicked in; and in his groin—when I went to pick him up, I tell you ... there was a lump big as ... I'm not kidding ... big as that fist. Does that sound reasonable? Does that sound like self-defence?

LUKIE. Sounds like one side of a story, but we don't know the circumstances, do we?

CLARRY. I know this: if anything happens to that kid, I tell you straight, it'll be murder.

LUKIE. You're a step ahead, Jack.

CLARRY. That's what I said; murder!

LUKIE [*topping him*]. And take a tip; don't drink any more of that stuff. Sort of blurs your values. [*They look at each other*

[73]

*for a caged moment.*] Well, I don't see myself in a beard, but I promised the wife I'd play Father Christmas for the kids . . .

CLARRY [*desperately*]. Listen . . . what's your name again?

LUKIE. Lukie, Detective-Sergeant.

CLARRY. Listen, Lukie; for . . . for the love of Christ, what do I tell 'em?

LUKIE. Wish I could help you, Jack. Yeah, I wish I could help you.

> [*He exits.* CLARRY, *after a blurred moment follows him, puzzled, to the sideway.*

CLARRY [*quietly*]. You better. You better try, Lukie. Yeah you better try 'cos you . . . you're a servant, d'ya hear, Lukie? A civil bloody servant . . . and you better be civil.

> [*The speech has built in intensity, finishing in a shout.* MOMMA *appears at the door.*

MOMMA. Clarry . . . ? Is that poppa. Is he come?

CLARRY [*shamed*]. Some galah, singing out there. Got on me nerves.

> [MARIA, *her manner vague as she fights against the drug, stumbles out of the door. She wears* MOMMA'S *old slippers.*

MARIA. Poppa . . . ? Where is he . . . ? Where . . . ?

MOMMA. 'S not poppa; not yet.

MARIA. But . . . I thought I heard . . .

CLARRY. Look now, you're supposed to be lying down.

MARIA. Thought I heard him.

MOMMA. Clarry's right; you should lie down. Come.

MARIA. Blankets are hot. In there, everything's so . . . sticky.

CLARRY. Never mind.

[74]

MARIA. Cool here; you can breathe.

CLARRY [*taking her arm*]. Come on. Inside.

MARIA. You heard me. I want to stay out here.

MOMMA. Maria.

MARIA. Why don't you leave me alone? Why do you want to . . .

CLARRY [*holding her firmly*] Nobody "wants to", anything darl; you just gotta take things easy, that's all. [*She is looking at him; he almost smiles and tenderly moves a sweat-wet strand of hair from her forehead.*] I know. I know how you feel.

MARIA [*looks steadily at him for a long moment, then quietly*]. Next time you're up the street, you buy yourself a medal.

[*She breaks from* CLARRY. MOMMA *moves to follow her.* CLARRY *intervenes.*]

CLARRY. She's off your bed. It means you can turn in, anyway, mumma.

MOMMA. Me? I'm not tired.

CLARRY. You can't do no good hanging about.

MOMMA. Maybe no; but jussa same, I like to stay.

MARIA [*with a wan smile*]. Losing your touch, aren't you boss?

[*Her tone to* CLARRY *is faintly derisive; especially in the abbreviation of his name.*] Don't let it worry you. Pour yourself another drink, Cla. Pour one for momma, too.

MOMMA. Mmmmmm?

MARIA. Make her drunk. Maybe she'd talk even funnier . . . or walk a tight-rope . . . or drop dead. Good old Momma Macaroni! Anything for a laugh, eh, Cla?

CLARRY. She's half-dopey. I think I better take her home.

MARIA. Take me home? You booked a ship?

CLARRY. Look, what's the matter with you?

MARIA. You take me to Italy?

MOMMA. Maria; gentle; gentle.

MARIA [to CLARRY]. Italia, that's my home, tell your mother, and don't you ever forget it either.

MOMMA. Maria, baby; no more; no more to talk like this. Not now. 'S not good for you; 's not good for the little bambino.

CLARRY [with an attempt at lightness]. Yeah, take it easy, willya? I got an interest in that warehouse, too, you know.

MOMMA [smiles]. Alaways, Clarry, he puts things so funny.

MARIA. Reg'lar Ginger Meggs.

MOMMA. You like Ginger Meggs? Never you don't say what you want. You like little boy baby, uh? Or maybe little girl baby, uh?

MARIA. Boy? Girl? I don't care, Momma, one way or the other.

MOMMA. Ooooh, Maria, that's not good thing to say. If a momma don't care, who does care?

CLARRY [shakes his head at MOMMA]. 'Course she cares. She's just tired, that's all.

MOMMA. You know what I think for you? Little boy; 'cos boy's good for business too.

CLARRY [grins]. Fowler and Son. [To MARIA.] Yeah; how about that?

MARIA. How about Fowler and Bianchi?

MOMMA. Maria . . .

MARIA. That's *not* good for business, is it? Foreigners, Momma. Out! Gotta keep it local.

MOMMA. Maria . . . I think . . .

MARIA. Well, it's about time, Momma. *Finalemente!* It's about time you thought. And me; I've been thinking too . . . the number of times I've been with him, Momma . . . [*she points to* CLARRY] . . . when he's introduced Gino to people, but never once did he call him his brother-in-law.

CLARRY. What're you talking about?

MARIA. Have you?

CLARRY. Because it didn't come up that way. Look darl, I know how you feel.

MARIA. You know . . .

CLARRY. So give me a chance; take it easy, willya?

MARIA. "Take it easy." What . . . so I can deliver you a fat, healthy, kickable baby?

MOMMA [*with pain*]. Maria . . .!

MARIA. Well, don't bank on it, you hear me? 'Cos I haven't delivered yet.

MOMMA. Santa Maria . . .

MARIA. And the way I feel now, I'm not sure I want to . . .

MOMMA. Maria! Maria, why you talk like this tonight?

MARIA [*turning on* MOMMA]. Tonight? *Dio Santo!* You don't know. Years of nights; years and years. Oh, it's about time you thought, Momma. You go into that little shop on the corner, and that drunk-dazed twitching shell of a man looks down on you, and you stand there and let him call you names. Let *him*—that wreck, who calls himself a good Australian—

let him judge *you*. You know what you should do? You should spit in his face.

CLARRY [*placating*]. Look darl, slow down, willya?

MARIA. Spit in his drunken face.

CLARRY. You're working yourself up over nothing.

MARIA [*turning on him*]. Nothing! His brother-in-law is lying in hospital and . . .

CLARRY. All right, then; not nothing. I keep trying to tell you . . .

MOMMA. Please; please. I can't take much more like this.

MARIA. *You* can't. You think you're alone? Every day more of us are coming . . . every day the same . . . suspicion . . . resentment . . . [CLARRY *turns away*.] He doesn't understand. But you don't have to, do you Cla? 'Cos you're top boy; it's us . . . *we've* got to understand *you*.

CLARRY [*violently*]. Will you listen? I keep trying to tell you . . .

MARIA [*full in* CLARRY's *face*]. No! You listen. I tell you if it's a boy, you know what I'm going to call him? Gino. You hear that? Gino!

CLARRY [*breaking from her*]. I'm trying to tell you; you won't even listen.

MARIA [*to* MOMMA]. You see? He knows. He knows what that'd mean.

MOMMA. But Gino's nice name; good name.

MARIA. Is it? Look. Look at his face. He knows. It's a good name, Momma, but not good enough to save it from the boot.

CLARRY. Maria, for the . . .

MARIA. Don't get het up, Cla., that was just a big joke, 'cos you'll see, won't you, ours'll be called Tom, or Bill, or Jack; some good Aussie name, so he can play with Aussie kids and he'll grow up like a good Aussie—with solid stone for a heart!

[*To* CLARRY.] But I tell you this . . .

MOMMA. No, Maria; you say too much.

MARIA. If anything happens to him . . . I know whose fault it will be.

MOMMA. Stop. No. Stop. STOP!!

[*Silence.* MARIA *sags on to the bench.*

MARIA. Floor's all yours, Cla.

MOMMA. Please, for momma; you come inside and rest, uh?

MARIA [*looks at her, smiling sadly*]. Poor little Momma. Poor lost little Momma.

[*She shudder-sighs like the after-effects of a deep, bitter attack of tears.*

MARIA [*slowly checking*]. Momma; the tree. It's gone.

MOMMA. No, Maria . . .

MARIA. It's not there.

MOMMA. Clarry; he just . . .

MARIA [*swinging on him*]. Where is it? What have you done with it?

CLARRY. I haven't done nothing . . .

MARIA [*pushing past him*]. You got no right to touch it.

CLARRY. Touch it! I pulled down the stinking blind, that's all.

[MARIA *releases the blind, and it rolls clacketing over and over and over.*

MOMMA. There; now we see it again; now we come inside, uh?

[79]

MARIA [*breaking from her*]. Why did you let him pull that down? Are you ashamed of it, too?

MOMMA. Ashamed?

CLARRY. Look, you're behaving like an idiot.

MARIA [*to* CLARRY]. Forgive and forget, so we pull down the blind, uh? Se we don't see no more how wicked . . . wicked, cruel you can be.

CLARRY. For the love of Christ will you cut it out? [*He takes her roughly by the arms and shakes her; yelling*] NOW WILL YOU CUT IT OUT!!!

> [*They are on the veranda. There is a deep controlled silence; then slowly, slowly,* POPPA *emerges from the sideway entrance and into the yard.*

MOMMA. Poppa . . .? You don't ring . . .

> [POPPA *takes her slowly in; and reaches for her hand.*

MOMMA. He's . . . all right . . . Poppa?

> [*He smiles, pressing her hand to his lips—not kissing it—but holding it against his mouth.*

MOMMA. Maria; Maria, Madre Santa. *Ti ringrazio.* You hear Maria? He's all right. Gino, he's all right.

> [MARIA *stunned, crosses herself in a quick automatic gesture.*

CLARRY. Didn't I tell you? Didn't I say . . .? [*He rushes for the side fence.*]

> [MOMMA *only now realizes—hot tears against her hand—that* POPPA *is crying.*

MOMMA. Poppa . . .? Poppa, what for? Not now; you don't

[80]

cry now. Look I gotta something for you. Guess what I got
for you? Look. .[*She takes out the harmonica.*] 'S all right;
Poppa . . . no more . . .

MARIA. Poppa . . . ? [*There is apprehension in the call.*] Poppa . . .
why don't you say something? Tell us . . . [*She comes slowly
down the steps.*] Words, Poppa; find the words. [*The last few
yards she rushes.*] Poppa . . . Poppa . . . look at me.

[*He can't.*

MARIA. Look at me; look, LOOK!

[*She takes his face roughly between her hands, reading the
truth from its lines . . . holding the pain between her palms.
CLARRY is behind her. Slowly she backs away.*

No; no . . . Poppa . . . no!

MOMMA [*apprensive now*]. Poppa . . . ?

MARIA [*an animal, anguished plea*]. No . . . [*She turns to run and
is in CLARRY'S arms.*]

CLARRY. Maria; no come on; take hold of yourself.

[*But it is too late. Control has gone.*

MARIA. No . . . no . . . [*She struggles to free herself.*] He's dead.
Dead. DEAD! Take your hands . . . let me go . . . go . . .
let me . . . take your . . . you killed him . . . KILLED HIM.
YOU . . . KILLED . . . HIM. . . .

[*She is attacking him now with nails and feets and words,
the agony running from her with the tears. MOMMA
stands benumbed. POPPA quietly weeps. MARIA cries uncontrollably struggling, fighting, until CLARRY strikes her a
swift, stinging blow across the face. Time stops. She
stares at him, uncomprehending . . . slowly backs away,
and then in one quick movement, she turns and doubles,*

*clutching at her stomach. In a second* CLARRY *has her in his arms, stumbling towards the house.*

THE CURTAIN BEGINS TO FALL

*But* MARIA, *quietly moaning, grabs at the veranda post.* CLARRY *remonstrates;* MOMMA *advances; pleading, crying through her own tears, trying to free* MARIA'S *hands . . . trying until we can't see them any more.*

# ACT III

TIME: *Christmas Day : 7 a.m. and already the sun has settled to a gentle warmth.*

*The stage is empty, but not tidy—for the garbage which* POPPA *deposited over the fence* R. *the previous night has now been returned, and lies strewn about the yard.*

[*A moment, and* POPPA *comes out on to the veranda wearily drying his face and head—which he has just held under the tap. He wears no shirt—only a yellowing wool vest. He stops at the sight of the yard, and in the street outside, a group of excited children rush laughing past the house and down the hill.*

*He puts the towel on the end of the bed, and at the same time sees the mouth-organ. He picks it up from the bed, comes down into the yard, extracts the broom from beneath the house, but instead of sweeping, he lifts the harmonica to his lips . . . just at this moment the remnants of the rubbish comes over the fence* R.—*two large cabbage leaves landing like a heavy afterthought. The mouth-organ drops amid the rubbish . . . and with slow, almost controlled care* POPPA *grinds it, and grinds and grinds it out of shape with his heel.*

MOMMA [*calling : off*]. Poppa . . . [*She appears at the kitchen door.*]

POPPA [*roughly ; without looking at her*]. I don't want to see you out here.

[83]

MOMMA. The towel from the kitchen, you take it?

POPPA. Promise: promise: what'sa the good? You promise me to sleep. It's only seven o'clock. I don't want to see you.

MOMMA. Inside's too hot to sleep.

POPPA. Front door's got hinges, like always.

MOMMA [*puts a comforting hand on his shoulder*]. It's open . . .
[*She sits beside him*] . . . but I don't know if the doctor he wants me; and anyway . . . I just lie there. Alla night I lie there and I see them floating by like a picture; all those lovely years, all gone.

> [*They are sitting together on the step: two wrinkled help-less children, in the new, early silence. A moment and the children outside scream up the hill.*

What you do here, uh? How you come to make this mess?

POPPA [*rising and taking up the broom*]. They don't like my present I give to them.

MOMMA. They don't like? That's good. What about us, uh?
[*Control is going; and she turns to attack the fence* R.] What about us?

POPPA. Momma . . .

MOMMA. How you like our present, uh? How you like to see *your* blood running . . . twenty-one yearsa your blood running . . . running . . . How you like that for a present, uh?

> [*The words are pushing from her in a sort of tired agony, and now she snatches up the refuse aiming it viciously at the fence* R. *screaming.*

Porci! E colpa vostra, vostra, mi sentite? E per questo vi odiero! odiero per il resto della mia vita.

POPPA. No, Momma, NO. NO!!!

[*During this* LEILA *has appeared helplessly watching from the upstairs window.*

LEILA [*commanding*]. Sh! Quiet. You gotta be quiet.

POPPA [*holding* MOMMA *and her pain*]. 'S all right Mrs. Pratt. 'S all right. 'S all right.

LEILA. You got some spare energy, you can chip a bit more ice for the doc; okay?

POPPA. Soon. She bring it soon. [LEILA *disappears*.] Then you gotta have a rest too . . . She don't hear. She got troubles, too, and yet alla night to sit up with Maria like that. Momma. Your nose drips.

MOMMA [*sniffing*]. And that Clarry, I could . . . [*She shakes her head.*] Why he don't come back, uh? Just now he *should* be here.

POPPA. You want me to go look for him?

MOMMA. Where, uh? No; if he don't wanna to come back . . .

POPPA. Last night, what she say: that hurt him, Momma.

MOMMA. And him: don't he hurt back? To hit her . . . !

POPPA [*looks up at the window which now symbolizes their future*]. But she *shoulda* gone to hospital like he say. There, they got everything: if something go wrong . . .

MOMMA [*covering his mouth with her hand*]. You don't say that. We have enough go wrong, you hear? From now on, nothing go wrong no more.

DONNY [*calling : off*]. Leil . . .? Are you there, Leil?

MOMMA. Tell him please, not to make no noise this morning.

[*She exits into the house. During the next* POPPA, *with hands and broom replaces the rubbish in the bin.*

DONNY [*calling off*]. You there, Leil?

[85]

POPPA. Mr. Pratt? Sh . . .! No noise please, no noise this morning.

DONNY [*appearing over the fence*]. Oerh, g'day, Pop. [*His reactions are slowed by alcholic muzz and pain.*] Seen the missus?

POPPA. She's upstairs—with Maria.

DONNY. Oerh, I'm like an outlaw. I dunno, look, honest, last night did I make's big fool of meself as Leil's trying to make out?

POPPA. You don't remember?

DONNY. Scouts Honour. Like she says: I must soak it up like rotten blottin' paper.

POPPA. You don't remember, 's all right, eh, Mr. Pratt? You don't remember, it don't happen, uh?

DONNY. That's what I keep trying to tell her, but she don't listen. Gee, she shook me this morning, though, about young . . . you know, I dunno what the world's coming to. Kid like that. . . I liked him, too . . . sorta friendly, you know, and . . .

POPPA. I call Mrs. Pratt for you.

DONNY. Er—Pop—er look, could I ask a favour? Could I come through? I mean: she's so bloomin' sore, and . . . when you're in somebody else's place, I mean . . . you know, it's sorta like having a referee, like.

POPPA. Sure; sure; you come through if you want to.

DONNY. Oerh, you're a sport, Pop.

POPPA [*calling, softly up*]. Mrs. Pratt . . .?

DONNY [*quickly disappearing*]. Hey, give us a go.

POPPA [*calling*]. Are you there, Mrs. Pratt?

LEILA [*appearing at the bedroom window*]. What've I done now?

POPPA. Mrs. Pratt, I think's time you have a break now, uh?

[MOMMA *appears behind her at the window.*

[86]

All night in that room; you need fresh air.

MOMMA. Poppa's right.

LEILA. Yeah; ta-ta.

MOMMA. I stay with Maria. [*To* POPPA.] She comes.

LEILA. Honest . . .! I dunno . . .! [*She disappears.*]

POPPA. Momma? The doctor; what does he say?

    [MOMMA *simply looks, and slowly she closes the window.*

DONNY [*his head appearing through the palings*]. Okay? Can I come through?

POPPA. Mmmm? Yes. She be down in a minute; it's better I leave you alone.

DONNY [*reluctantly*]. Well . . . yeah . . . yeah.

POPPA. You don't be scared, Mr. Pratt. All you need's a little courage . . . but not the kind you have last night, uh?

    [*He exits into the house.* DONNY *waits a moment in nervous indecision, then dives up the sideway as* LEILA *comes out of the house. She stretches, coming down into the yard; looks up; worriedly down as the smell of the garbage bins reaches her and quickly she takes out and lights a cigarette. A second later* DONNY *strides down the sideway.*

DONNY [*with forced animation*]. There y'are, Leil! I been looking all over.

LEILA. Whatta you think you're doing in here?

DONNY. Nothing; I—just wondered where *you* was, that's all.

LEILA. Well, now you know you can just turn round and sail right out again.

DONNY. What's up?

LEILA. Hmph! Look at me eye, and say that.

[87]

DONNY. Eh?

LEILA. Look at it. Black. That's all.

DONNY. No it's not.

LEILA. Go on. Tell me now you never hit me.

DONNY. Well, like, I didn't.

LEILA. May Gawd forgive you for the stinking liar that you are. Get out.

DONNY. Like I keep saying: how can I a hit you if I don't remember?

LEILA. I don't want you in here causing more trouble. Get out.

DONNY. Aaaah, whatta you talking about, trouble?

LEILA. You heard me: now get.

DONNY [*hesitates*]. What about breakfast?

LEILA. Kid you're on a diet.

DONNY. I'll get it, I mean.

LEILA. You?

DONNY. I could boil you'n egg, if you like.

LEILA. Yeah, and I could tell you what to do with it.

DONNY. Aaaah, look, Leil . . .

LEILA. Every lousy Christmas, that's all I get; aaah, look, Leil . . . Well Leil's seen enough this Christmas to make her sick and rotten tired of looking. Leil's gunna do a bit of duck-shoving herself: Leil's gunna buy a few new clothes; get out a bit; kick a leg; see how you like it.

DONNY [*patiently*]. I could scramble it.

LEILA. You can sit in it for all I care. Now get out.

DONNY. You won't even give a man a chance to explain.

LEILA. I'll explain you. First thing after the holiday's over you'll

[88]

explain your way into Town and if it costs you thirty-rotten-quid you're going to buy me a milk-jug like the one you smashed on me last night. Understand?

DONNY. I was gunna get it anyway; sort of a surprise.

LEILA. Stick your surprises; all I want's me milk-jug. Now get out.

DONNY. Gawd, you're a hard woman, Leil.

LEILA. Yeah. Ta-ta.

DONNY. Hard as rotten nails.

> [*He exits through the fence.* LEILA *stamps out her cigarette, and moves to exit as* MOMMA *emerges on to the veranda.*

MOMMA [*stopping her*]. The Doctor, he don't want us. He don't want nobody, he say, till Maria decide to give in.

DONNY [*appearing over the fence*]. A cuppa tea then, Leil . ..? Oerh, g'day, Mrs. B.

LEILA. Look, you're a nuisance: a drunken nuisance. Now will you go away before I throw something at your stupid-looking head.

DONNY [*disappears*]. You're a hard woman, Leil.

MOMMA. You shouldn't talk to him like that.

LEILA. You should try being married to him. [*She holds her face up to* MOMMA.] Can you see any colour there?

MOMMA. Mmm? She's red; just here.

LEILA. Feels like it should be black.

MOMMA. No black.

LEILA. Not even round the edges? [MOMMA *shakes her head.*] You're sure?

MOMMA. You *want* it to be black?

LEILA. Well, I don't want him to think he's got away with it, that's all.

> [MOMMA *looks anxiously up at the window.*

MOMMA. 'S not good to take so long as this.

LEILA. You know how it is; some take it easy, some take it tough.

MOMMA [*quietly*]. 'S more than that. She don't want it.

LEILA. What?

MOMMA. The baby. She don't want it.

LEILA. That's a terrible thing to say.

MOMMA [*Stopping her*]. She don't want to give it up. I know! I'm her momma. And I know. Why? Because this is mine, she say; this baby's mine, and I don't share him with nobody who treats him like they treat my brother. She rather even it die! Die!!! You hear? And she die, too!

> [*A dull agonized scream comes from the upstairs window; it resolves to a choke as the two women race to the door; reaching it as* POPPA *comes rushing out.*

POPPA. Momma; Momma; Mrs. Pratt ... quick ... quick ...

> [*He is pushed aside.* MOMMA *bustling past him first, followed by* LEILA, *then* POPPA. *A second later* POPPA *is coming out backwards through the door—forced out by* LEILA.

LEILA. Now we had this out before. We want you, we'll ring.

> [*She disappears, leaving* POPPA *to shift nervously along the veranda. Then he rushes into the yard and to the window says in a barely audible voice—*

POPPA. You want something, you let me know? And anything happen you soon tell me ... I gotta to know what ... [*His hands meet and he turns from the window.*] You tell me ....

[*A stone propelled down the sideway strikes the metal garbage can. This has a steadying effect on* POPPA, *then he snatches up the broom, and mumbling moves to the sideway.*]

Kids! You kids, shoo; you hear me. Shoo; no games today; quiet today. . . .

[*He is met by* CLARRY *who slops wearily into the yard.*]
[*Gratefully.*] Clarry, thank God you come back; Maria, she . . . [*Then he remembers.*] But . . . where you been all night . . .uh?

CLARRY. Out. [*Silently moves to pick up the stone, but his right hand is stiff and bruised. He picks the stone up with his left, holding his right under his left armpit.*]

POPPA. 'S fine thing you do . . .

CLARRY [*firmly*]. Get off me back, Pop. I warn you; I'm in no mood for a ride.

POPPA. You, uh? You in no mood? What about others?

CLARRY. And I don't want to be read no lectures.

POPPA. Your wife. You don't care about her . . .? 'Bout what she goes through . . .?

CLARRY. Shut up. . . .

POPPA. . . . and momma; first Gino, now Maria, and you say . . .

CLARRY. Shut up!

POPPA. . . . you in no mood!

CLARRY [*flinging the stone viciously against the fence* R.]. You heard what I said. SHUT UP!

[POPPA *sees and grabs at the extended, blood-congealed fist.*]

POPPA. What's this? What you do to your hand?

[CLARRY *relaxes.*]

Clarry, answer me: what happens?

[91]

CLARRY [*screws the fist away from his grasp*]. I been writing letters.

POPPA [*he looks at* CLARRY'S *back . . . and recognizes defeat*]. You had some breakfast?

[CLARRY *shakes his head.*

I better fix for you something.

CLARRY. Don't think I could swallow it, Pop.

POPPA [*he checks at the door*]. Clarry, I know; I know how you feel, but please not to take it out on her. She's very sick girl, Clarry. Maybe I tell her you come back. . . .

CLARRY. I don't *want* you to tell her.

POPPA. Clarry, Clarry; all this pain, and who's hurt worst of all? It's you.

CLARRY. Not me, Pop; 'cos she put me back right where I was. Me? I'm just the old go-easy boy again.

POPPA. You gotta let me tell her something. One little message. [CLARRY *is silent.*] Look, you feel this way why you come back at all, uh?

CLARRY. I left me truck out there; me truck's me living. Pop . . . you can tell her—if she wants me . . . this time *she* sends the message.

[POPPA *exits into the house.* CLARRY *looks up at the window; moves wearily to the bed and flops on its side, his head sagging uncontrollably. Silence. Then the sound of children—shrill with the excitement of new-found toys.* CLARRY *flings himself from the veranda. Offstage, the children laugh in high-pitched squeals. He sags against the fence* R., *turns to face it, supporting himself—arms outstretched along its top. Then he brings his right fist down and painfully, wilfully begins to punch, and punch the fence. Each new punch squeezing gasps of uncontainable*

*pain from him.* LUKIE *appears at the sideway entrance—
as the upstairs window goes up and* LEILA *leans out.*

LEILA [*sharply*]. What the hell's going on down there? Are you
going mad, or what? We got a sick girl in here; sicker'n you'll
ever be; and she's gotta have quiet, d'y'understand? Now
either you shut up or you clear out; if you don't so help me, I'll
be down and I'll fix y'up myself.

[*She disappears;* LUKIE *wanders into view.*

LUKIE. We could find a place for her on the Force.

CLARRY [*quietly, deliberately*]. Get licked.

LUKIE. Charming. Must teach that to the children.

CLARRY. Get out, get out, or by Jeez, I'll . . .

LUKIE [*indicating the battered fist*]. What's the matter? Couldn't
you find a hammer? [CLARRY *turns stumbling towards the door.*]
Now look Jack . . .

CLARRY [*turning on him*]. No, it's your turn for looking. I don't
like you, Lukie; I don't like your wog name; I don't like your
flat face; I don't like your mouth or what comes out of it. In
fact, I don't like anything about you. Understand? So far as
I'm concerned you can get lost and stay there.

LUKIE [*pleasantly, as he saunters farther into the yard*]. That's
about the nicest character reading I ever had.

CLARRY. Quite a nut, aren't you, Lukie? But you don't fool me.
You don't fool me, Lukie; you just keep reminding me.

LUKIE. Of?

CLARRY. Hmph! Hearts and flowers. M for me Mother.

LUKIE. Now look, Jack.

CLARRY. The names not Jack. It's Clarry; short for Clarence.

[LUKIE *looks at him and snorts.*] Big joke; yeah.

[93]

LUKIE. Clarence, eh?

CLARRY. That's right; after the old man. It mighta suited him better; I dunno; we never met. A German—over there—got at him first; messed him up; messed him up for good.

LUKIE. Yeah . . . ?

CLARRY. So, she never forgot or forgive. Ever since then foreigners, any sort, so far as she was concerned, you could stick 'em. Put 'em in a big bag, so that blokes like you could drown 'em.

LUKIE. She's got a long memory . . .

CLARRY. Got a witness, too. [*He signifies Heaven, with a lift of his head.*] Keeps prodding Him every Sunday. Yeah; gets all dolled up, goes to Church, belts out the hymns; you know like Red and Yeller, Black and White, They're all precious in His sight; goes home, does the washing, and you'd never know the difference. Yeah, you two should get together. D'you sing, Lukie? I bet between you you'd raise the roof.

[MOMMA *comes out on to the veranda.*

MOMMA. Clarry! Clarry! 'S good you come now. But please, no more you don't knock on the fence like that; no noise. Clarry; we got to . . . [*She sees* LUKIE.] Oh, I'm sorry, I don't see you got a friend with you.

CLARRY. He's from the police, Momma.

MOMMA. Police? [*To* LUKIE.] About my boy? You come about Gino?

CLARRY [*to* LUKIE]. Why don't you run, Lukie? Isn't that what a good rat does?

LUKIE [*sharply*]. Look, I been pretty patient with you, son.

MOMMA. Clarry; please, why you talk like this? [*To* LUKIE.] Please . . . you say to me; what you come for?

[94]

LUKIE. Mrs. Bianchi? [MOMMA *nods*.] You'll be wanted on the twenty-eighth.

MOMMA. Wanted? What for?

LUKIE. The inquest.

MOMMA. In . . .? [*She looks at* CLARRY.] I don't understand . . . So many things I don't understand. You from the police; maybe you tell me; why they do this to my boy?

LUKIE. That's what the inquest's for; to find out. You'll have to wait till then, I'm afraid.

MOMMA [*impatiently*]. I don' wanna to wait. Now! I want to know now. They change this rule, all right . . but why for him? This his home. Never, never once does he say: Momma, letsa go home. Because for him here's home. Clarry . . .? That so, uh? You tell the man . . . you tell him. I got his papers say so. You wanna see his papers, when he go to the Town Hall? He shakes hands with the Mayor; he comes home to me and he says: Momma, look, and he got this big . . . what you say . . . certificate, uh? This we gotta put in a frame, he says. And he did, and's up there in that room, with his sister; now she there, too; she very sick girl, and all because . . . why? Why they do this? [*She is softly, imploringly crying.*]

[POPPA *appears at fly-screen door.*

LUKIE. The twenty-eighth. You'll remember that, will you?

CLARRY. She remembers; she forgets; what the hell difference will it make?

MOMMA. Please, please: I wanna to understand. I try; so hard I try. Is . . . maybe . . . because he talk different, uh? 'S at it?

POPPA [*enters on to veranda*]. Momma . . .

MOMMA. Is that his fault? God says . . . not us . . . no man says where he can be born.

[95]

POPPA. Momma; no; no; shshshshsh . . .

MOMMA. But why he don't tell me? Nobody they don't tell me.

[*Suddenly vicious.*] I tell you; I find the people who do this to my boy, I make a them suffer.

POPPA. No, Momma . . .

MOMMA. Suffer, you hear me? Like they make him suffer. These people no good. I spit: spit . . . like Maria say . . . spit on these people. And hate. I hate. Hate! You hear me. I HATE.

POPPA. No, Momma; Momma; shshshshsh . . . Maria, shshsh.

MOMMA. But to kick him, Poppa; kick—like an animal . . . [*Faintly.*] 'Scusa . . . I think . . . I be sick. [*She exits stumbling into the house.*]

CLARRY [*to* LUKIE]. You must be feeling on top of the world.

LUKIE [*to* POPPA]. You the father?

POPPA. Si.

LUKIE. I tried to tell your wife. The inquest is on the twenty-eighth. You understand that? [POPPA *nods.*] We have to wait till the Coroner's had *his* little say before we lay official charges, but . . .

POPPA. Please?

LUKIE. We booked eight last night. Arrested three of 'em.

POPPA. Arrest . . . ?

LUKIE. And we found a girl, too; arranged to meet him in the foyer. Saw most of it happen, she says . . . so we'll probably call her to cut down on the provocation angle.

POPPA. You gonna to punish these people?

LUKIE. They'll get whatever the Judge says. Why?

POPPA. I just wonder. They punish us. We punish them . . . [*And he shakes his head at the utter uselessness of it*] 'Scusa, I must see to my wife.

[*He exits. And in the pause* CLARRY *surveys the other man.*

LUKIE. Well, we're supposed to be on our way to Rosebud for a picnic. You like Rosebud?

CLARRY [*not unpleasantly*]. What do they call that: copper's cunning? Why the change of face, eh? After promotion?

LUKIE. I'm happy. [*Pause.*] But I got a boss with ambitions.

CLARRY. I thought so!

LUKIE. Yeah; just the genius of the working class, aren't you.

CLARRY. And you? What are you?

LUKIE [*shrugs*]. Just a civil servant . . . losing out on valuable swimming time. [*He moves to the sideway.*]

CLARRY. Lukie! While you're down the beach, do me a favour? [*Pleasantly.*] Drown.

LUKIE [*shakes his head*]. Sorry, Jack; doesn't go with my character. Oh, and one last thing, don't do it again. Call mine a wog name. It's good honest-to-God German. [*Grins.*] *Should* meet up with your Mum sometime, like you say. We could maybe work up a duet for the Amateur hour.

[*He exits up the sideway; and* LEILA'S *head comes furtively out from the house. She goes immediately to the veranda-edge and looks off after the retreating figure. She carries an enamel dish with used gauze, etc. in it.*

LEILA. What was footsy after?

CLARRY. Not you, screamer; nor Superman in there. You're safe.

LEILA [*she jerks her head to the fence, right*]. Wouldn't put it

[97]

past old Mudguts to have a go at us. And disturbing the peace . . . that's right up her alley.

CLARRY. Disturbing it? He was having a bash at destroying it altogether.

LEILA [*wearily*]. Save me legs, Cla. Stuff this in the bin for me, willya?

CLARRY. I'll buy you a little black boy on the way.

LEILA [*seeing his bloodied fist*]. Whatta you done to your hand?

CLARRY [*dismissing it*]. Caught it in the mincer. Give's it.

LEILA. Don't be a damn' fool; mincer . . .!

CLARRY. Do you want it emptied or not?

[*Watched by* LEILA, *he takes the gauze and deposits it in the garbage can, checks, and takes up a small object lying near by.*

LEILA. Had your breakfast?

[CLARRY *thoughtfully pockets the object.*

You look like a torn advert. When 'ud you eat last?

CLARRY. All these questions. You should be Chairman of the Quiz kids.

LEILA. You tell me nothing, how else can I find out?

CLARRY [*tired and impatient*]. Do us a favour; don't play the shrewdie, Leil.

LEILA. Mmmmm?

CLARRY. You think I don't know? She's been tearing me apart all night. You think I don't know?

LEILA [*firmly*]. She's been *delirious* all night. The only thing she's been tearing apart is herself. 'Cos she's scared, Cla: scared, like she'd thought you'd run out on her.

CLARRY. How's that for a laugh? I'll tell you who did the

[98]

running. She did. You shoulda seen her. Yeah, she streaked away.

LEILA. Did you try and stop her?

CLARRY. Nothing woulda stopped her. Nothing.

LEILA. Did you try.

CLARRY. Nothing, I tell you. Not even that.

LEILA [*looking at the extended, bloodied fist*]. Seems like it was gent's night all round.

CLARRY [*has risen to the veranda post*]. Look; see these marks? That's her fingernails, where she grabbed it when I tried to carry her in . . . and screamed; wouldn't let go; wouldn't even let me take her to the hospital . . . So I . . . [*He holds up the fist and shakes a lost head*] . . . I tried to take her into her mother's room . . . she just screamed . . . running . . . running all the time; even holding her in my arms she was running . . . till she made me carry her up there . . . to *his* room. Then she stopped. And that's the answer, I reckon. While she had him, she needed me around too. Now he's gone . . .

LEILA. She'll need you double, I reckon.

CLARRY. Yeah? Well, when she does she'll have to say it.

LEILA. You're making it tough, Cla.

CLARRY. That's right. Now let it rest, willya, Leil? [*Pause; then almost to himself; lost.*] You live with someone, think you understand them, and all the time they're thinkin' things you never even knew. [*He looks up.*] But last night—it clicked for me. I dunno . . . I felt sort of . . . good, and I wanted to tell her, Leil; tell her I knew what was going on inside her; and I tried, and all she did was slam the door in my face. [*He looks at the mashed fist, lost.*] Where's the answer? I dunno.

LEILA. Well, don't look at me. Wedding ring and a game of chase-y, that's all I got, so don't look at me.

CLARRY [*almost lightly, as he stirs himself*]. I don't see you doing much chasing.

LEILA. Me? I gave up years ago. I was too far out in front.

[*She is at the door now, but hesitates and comes quietly back.*

When I got married, Cla—I had tickets on myself then—I went out and I bought myself a pair of the highest heels I could find. You shoulda seen me. Like a mast I looked. And in the church there, I found I was so tall I had to look down at him; and . . . you know how things go through your mind; well I remember like it was yesterday, thinking: Gawd you're smaller'n I am, and . . . funny, but from that day he never seemed to grow any bigger.

[*Pause, then* DONNY'S *voice comes over the fence* L.

DONNY [*off*]. Leil . . .? Is that you, Leil . . .?

LEILA. Show your drunken face over this fence again, and I'm warning you: I'll throw something at it.

DONNY [*off*]. Where'd you put the sugar, Leil?

LEILA. Oh, up in Annie's room.

DONNY [*off*]. Where?

LEILA. Use your bloodshot eyes, and look.

DONNY [*fading*]. Gawd, you're a hard woman, Leil.

LEILA [*Pause, to* CLARRY]. Those high heels, Cla, was the biggest mistake I ever made. [*She pats his shoulder.*] So take it easy boy, eh?

[POPPA *emerges on to the veranda.*

POPPA. Mrs. Pratt . . .?

LEILA. Yeah, Pop; yeah, I'm shirking it, aren't I?

POPPA. No; no; just momma's not well, so anything you need, you calla me, uh?

LEILA [*to* CLARRY]. I wouldn't have told you all that but—take it easy, willya, Cla, 'cos just now you're looking dangerously tall to me.

[*She exits into the house.*

CLARRY. She'll be writing books next.

POPPA. I fry some salami for you; you eat it now?

CLARRY [*shakes his head*]. Turn out the gas, Pop.

POPPA. You should eat.

CLARRY. Yeah, sharks should fly.

POPPA. What kinda thing's that to say? You got a mouse in your head, today, or what?

CLARRY. What, Pop. That's it. Just a little hunk a "what", Humph! So what happens now?

POPPA. The Priest comes. I promise momma to put a shirt on.

CLARRY. No, when you leave here. Where'll you go? Home again.

POPPA. Home. Here's home. Here's our friends.

CLARRY. Friends! God Almighty, they kill your son and you call 'em friends.

POPPA. Sh! Clarry; not too loud. And you wrong; not our friends, they don't kill. Not Mrs. Pratt, and the rest.

CLARRY. Plenty of others. Plenty more to kill—and their killing children.

POPPA. Children. They don't know what they do.

CLARRY. Don't know! Good, Holy...! Are you weak as well as stupid? Like mumma says: you should hate these people.

POPPA. And you see what hate does to momma. Makes her stomach sick.

[101]

CLARRY. So you're gonna be a warrior, eh? Stay here and battle it out?

POPPA [*simply*]. I look like what you say . . . warrior? But battle, there I think you right. There's big battle coming, Clarry. So you don't worry about me, uh? You worry about yourself.

CLARRY. What've I got to worry about?

POPPA. Soon you gotta make up your mind, Clarry.

CLARRY. I don't know what you're talking about.

POPPA. You know—very well, you know.

CLARRY. I'm telling you . . .

POPPA [*impatiently*]. Don't fight me this morning, Clarry, 'cos this morning I'm full to here, and I maybe don't know what I say.

CLARRY. Say what you like. Let's all have a go.

POPPA [*looks at him*]. Juss now you hate me; yes, you do . . . because once I say you our son, too. And that you don't like. 'Cos you don't want no wop for father, uh? No dirty dago. Oh, don't think I hurt myself; after last night, be a longa time before anything can hurt me again. But I can hurt you, Clarry, and that I got to do.

CLARRY. Well, ta . . .

POPPA. You know what I want to see from you Clarry? I want to see you cry. Yeah, you! From you I want to see one real tear. I want you have a pain inside a you so big that the shame don't matter. 'Cos then, only then, maybe, you'll understand.

CLARRY [*uncertainly*]. Well, you better sport yourself a camp-bed, Pop, you got a long wait.

POPPA [*in a sudden flash of temper*]. Why you fight yourself like this? What kinda animal are you? [*Pause.*] You see; you make me lose a my temper. But you can't run away no more,

Clarry, because when you took Maria, you took us; and what we are, so she is—and that you know when you marry her. You can't hide from it no more; you can't fight it.

CLARRY. I don't *wanna* fight. I don't wanna fight nothing. All I wanna do is live. Just—plain—live.

POPPA. And Gino, all he wanna do is dance; just to dance.

CLARRY. That was a dirty one, Pop.

POPPA. I said I got to hurt you. [*He takes the blooded fist.*] To hurt yourself, that's not enough, it's the someone else's pain that counts. And I got to show you that pain; and show you until I make you understand.

CLARRY. Make *me* understand? The way *you* talk . . . the way *she* talks, anyone'd think I married a whole damn' race. And all I did was get married like any other bloke.

POPPA. Then why you're not a father? Like any other bloke?

CLARRY. I'm not a doctor, neither; but I *shoulda* been a father. Twice, I shoulda been.

POPPA. But something went wrong. What mmm?

CLARRY. You know damn' well what.

POPPA [*nods*]. But do *you* know? She was afraid, Clarry; even before this happened last night, she was afraid . . . afraid what happen to Gino . . . happen to her babies, and yours. And I tell you, Clarry, if she go on thinking like that, you never gonna be a father as long as you live.

CLARRY [*looks, unbelievingly at him, then painfully aloud*]. Whadda youse want from me?

POPPA. A sign, that's all. Listen, why you think I ask you to take Gino into partners? That's a sign, that's all. Because it takes only one to start, Clarry; one to accept. 'Cos if you do then pretty soon your friend accept, then his friend, then . . .

CLARRY [*bewildered*]. Talk, talk, talk.

POPPA. But like all the rest, you only know what's good for your conscience to know. You gotta be big to say: this was my fault.

CLARRY. Mine? Was it *me* that kicked him?

POPPA [*quietly and with frightening simplicity*]. Clarry, it don't always need a boot to kick.

> [CLARRY *looks at him, incredulously.*

I got to hurt you, Clarry. [*Firmly.*]

CLARRY. Hurt me! Christ . . . [*He turns back, controlled.*] Look, ever since I walked down that sideway last night I was marked; marked by all of youse. Well, I'm sick of being the bunny, you hear? Sick of it.

POPPA. I don't say you kill . . .

CLARRY. You're right, you don't! 'Cos I'll tell you who killed. You did! *Your* mob! They can be bastards too. The *bad* in your *own* mob, that's who killed him. Whadda you think you are; a race of angels? You're the same as us; bad makes the mistakes, who pays? It's the good, same as us. You hear? Just THE SAME AS US!

> [CLARRY *has taken* POPPA *roughly by the vest. Now the full realization of this last statement strikes home to both of them.*
>
> POPPA *crumbles.* CLARRY, *lets the anger smooth from him and remembering, he extracts the broken harmonica from his pocket; putting it almost tenderly beside poppa. He moves towards the sideway.*

POPPA. Clarry . . . go up to her, Clarry, talk to her; tell her its gonna be all right.

CLARRY. I tried to tell her last night. [*He shakes his head*].

POPPA. Clarry . . .

CLARRY. See you, Pop.

POPPA [*lost*]. Clarry . . .! You leave us now, there's no hope for us. [*Sternly.*] You hear what I say? You go now, you don't come back.

> [CLARRY *takes a slow look about the yard, and exits up the sideway.* POPPA *is alone in the long, long silence . . . then the air is torn by the sound of a new baby's cry.* POPPA *stands transfixed, then rushes to the sideway where* CLARRY *has disappeared. He hesitates, moves quickly to the house, changes his mind, and rushes to the centre of the yard, calling up to the window.*

POPPA. Mrs. Pratt . . .? Mrs. Pratt . . .?

> [*He breaks off and rushes at the door as* MOMMA *comes out.*

MOMMA. You hear . . . You hear . . .?

POPPA [*calling*]. Mrs. Pratt . . .?

MOMMA. All night I lay awake to hear just one sound. Now I don't know if I hear it or not. Where you go?

POPPA. Up there, I gotta go up there.

MOMMA. You think I don't try? No, Poppa, no. Better to wait.

POPPA. Wait! Wait! How can I wait?

MOMMA. Wait. Wait. Clarry's with her; he tell us.

POPPA [*vaguely*]. Clarry . . .? Up there . . .? But . . .?

MOMMA. The front door's open like always. Already I'm on the stairs, Clarry comes flying past me like the wind, and . . . what's the matter?

POPPA [*shaking his head*]. Whadda you know, uh? Talk; talk; talk; like he say. Alla that breath, and I got a voice no bigger than one tiny little baby's.

> [*The window shoots up and* LEILA *leans out.*

LEILA. Look, all the yelling; what do you think it is; a footy final, or what?

POPPA. I'm sorry, Mrs. Pratt.

LEILA. I should think you are sorry, too. Just because you're a grandfather.

POPPA. Grand . . .?

LEILA. And as for you, Granny. Can't *you* keep him in check?

MOMMA [*softly*]. Granny . . .?

> [*They look at each other, the two old people; a slight, sad smile passes between them, and* MOMMA *reaches out to touch* POPPA.

LEILA. But I'm warning you; any more noise outa youse, and we'll send it straight back and get a refund. [*She disappears.*]

> [CLARRY *emerges from the house, nervous, drawn, but controlled.*

POPPA. Clarry . . .! To use the front way. That's to cheat.

CLARRY [*finally focussing*]. Whadda you know. I'm a father.

POPPA. Me, too, and momma; and Maria? Clarry, Marie?

> [CLARRY *nods, emotion now gathering weight in his head.*

MOMMA [*a little animal pain*]. Maria, Madre Santa . . .!

POPPA. You saw her?

CLARRY. Only for a minute; over the Doctor's shoulder, like; then she said something, and he shoved me out.

MOMMA. What? What she say?

CLARRY. I couldn't hear very well, but it sounded like . . . sorta like: forgive me. [*He turns away, gently tiredly laughing.*] Jesus, eh? [*And painfully the tears begin.*]

[106]

POPPA [*stopping* MOMMA]. No, Momma; no.

[LEILA *bursts from the house with a bottle of beer and glasses which she shoves into* POPPA'S *arms.*]

LEILA. Here; quick, to wet its head. [*She exits.*]

MOMMA. She's like a whirl-a-wind.

POPPA [*offering her glass of beer*]. So . . . Momma . . .

MOMMA. Not me. You know, my stomach, it . . .

POPPA [*gently*]. Today you suffer, uh? [*He takes his glass from* CLARRY, *too.*]

MOMMA. And, Clarry, the bambino, uh? What it looks like, uh?

CLARRY. Bit squashed. Bit like pop.

POPPA [*proudly*]. Like a me.

MOMMA. Likea a him?

POPPA. Why not?

MOMMA. Why not? Nice thing to look like you, if she's a little girl.

[*And simultaneously, as* MOMMA *and* POPPA *look to* CLARRY, *they all realize that this is the one question still unanswered.*]

CLARRY. Jeez. I forgot to look!

[*As he races into the yard the window shoots up and* LEILA *appears.*]

LEILA. I'm with you . . . [*She holds out a glass.*] Surgical spirit. [*She gives a twitch.*] Me, 'n old Wilson'll be mates.

CLARRY. Hey, Leil, what is it? A him or a her?

LEILA. Competition, boy. It's a little bruiser.

CLARRY [*quietly*]. Boy, eh?

[MOMMA *hears this and moves to the bench down* L. *And during the next she sits, her back to the audience.*]

POPPA. You know what? [*Smiling to* MOMMA.] I think I'm gonna to paint this veranda.

LEILA. Whadda you gunna call him, Cla?

CLARRY. Give us a go. He's only just come.

LEILA. How about Clarence?

CLARRY. How about you dropping out that window?

POPPA. To my grandson—whatever his name.

CLARRY. Yeah, to [*he steadies*] Gino.

MOMMA [*with pain*]. Gino . . .

CLARRY. To young Gino. [*He drinks.*]

LEILA. Young Gino. [*She drinks.*]

POPPA [*looks at* MOMMA, *sitting alone, her shoulder's sagging and says very, very quietly* . . .] To Gino . . .

and

THE CURTAIN FALLS